A Christmas Eve Tale

About the Author

I have lived in Leeds most of my life, growing up in Rothwell and Woodlesford. I was a creative and daydreamy child with my head in the clouds most of the time. I loved performing on stage and joining local theatre companies.

I met my husband, Ian when I was just twenty, we've been together twenty-one years and we now have a four-year-old son called Max and our little rescued terrier dog, Bazil.

C. F. Draper

Illustrations by L. S. Rowe

A Christmas Eve Tale

Olympia Publishers
London

www.olympiapublishers.com
OLYMPIA PAPERBACK EDITION

A CIP catalogue record for this title is available from the British Library.

ISBN: 978-1-78830-426-9

First Published in 2019

Olympia Publishers
60 Cannon Street
London
EC4N 6NP
Printed in Great Britain

Dedication

For my beautiful son, Max Henry Draper, who sparks my imagination every day, and to Leah's beautiful boys, Aran and Ben.

May life be magical for you, always.

As you read this magical tale can you count the
number of mischievous mice?
Answer on the back page.

Once upon a time, in a house just like yours and mine stood a
beautiful and very large
Christmas tree.
The tree was so tall it almost touched the ceiling and its branches
were covered in the most wonderful decorations.

Every Christmas Eve something extraordinary would happen.
When the house was still and quiet, the decorations would come to life!

A Snowman that was hooked onto a branch stretched out
his arms and legs and yawned.
YAWnnnnn
Blinking and rubbing his eyes, he gazed around the room.
A wooden toy soldier stood to attention
and arranged his rifle.
A lantern switched on its light, sending
a warm glow around the room.
And at the top of the tree the Christmas tree fairy
fluttered her wings
sending a shower of silver glitter onto the presents below,
just like the first snow fall of winter.

The Snowman who was now fully awake
looked up at the Christmas tree fairy.
Maybe this year, thought the Snowman.
A wave of excitement came over him and his
eyes began to sparkle.

He unhooked himself from the
branch above and jumped down onto
the bauble below. Almost slipping
he grabbed some tinsel and hauled
himself up.

He had just a few hours in the night to reach the top of the tree before sunrise,
to be with his best friend,
the Christmas tree fairy.

Looking up
he could see her
smiling down at him,
she looked
a long way away
this year.

The owners of the tree had hung him much
lower down than usual and he wondered
if he would ever reach her.
Every year he would clamber up the tree,
climbing all obstacles
as he went.

Taking a deep breath,
he began his journey.
Stretching out his little legs
he hopped onto the next branch,
and the next and the next.
Passing a swinging star, a pine cone
dipped in gold paint and a bag of gold chocolate coins.

He eventually had to stop for he had come to a very old Christmas tree decoration. It was a small red and silver house. The Snowman had not seen this house before and he wondered if anyone lived there.
Looking in through the windows he could see Santa Claus.
Santa saw the Snowman and smiled, "Hello little Snowman," said Santa Claus. "What brings you to my house?"

"I was just passing by," said the Snowman. "I'm on my way to meet my best friend, the Christmas tree fairy."
"Ah I see," replied Santa, and how are you going to get all the way up there?" Pointing to the top of the tree. They both looked up and it was a very long way.
"Well," said the Snowman, the only way I know how, to climb up all the decorations, swinging myself up onto the branches and climbing up the tinsel."
"Sounds like a lot of hard work to me," said Santa.
"I only have a few hours left to get to the top," said the Snowman.

Meanwhile, at the top of the tree the Christmas fairy fluttered her wings and even more glitter shimmered down the tree, tiny sparkly flakes fell on Santa and the Snowman. The Snowman held out his hand to catch the falling stars, "See," said the Snowman.
"She knows I'm on my way."
"I hope you reach her before morning,"
said Santa.

The Snowman set off again, clambering over a Christmas cracker, his little legs sliding down the side of the red glistening paper.

He passed more baubles and bags of gold chocolate coins when suddenly, there in his path was a brand new Christmas tree decoration.

It was an ice skater and she wore a beautiful pink dress, her long legs stretched out beneath her and there on her feet were little pink skating boots. She looked sad.

"What's the matter?" asked the Snowman.

"I want to go ice skating," she replied, "But I'm stuck in this tree and I can't get down."

The Snowman replied, "Why don't you climb down the fairy lights, they lead to the floor?"

The ice skater looked at the Snowman and grinned. "They do!" she said in amazement. And grabbing hold of the wire she began to weave her way down the tree. "Thank you," she called as the Snowman peered down the tree.

The Snowman continued on his journey, he was almost
near the top when the wooden toy soldier appeared
from behind a glowing lantern.
"Who goes there?"
said the soldier in a booming voice.
"It's only me, the Snowman, I'm on my way to see my best friend."

"Not today!" responded the soldier.
"What do you mean?
I do this journey every year,"
replied the Snowman.
"What's different this year?"
"Captain's orders," boomed the soldier.
"I cannot allow anyone to walk any
further on this branch because it's about to
break in two."
"Oh, I see," replied the Snowman.
"Well I'll just have to climb up
this tinsel instead."
"I'll give you a leg up,"
said the soldier.

The Snowman reached
the end of the tinsel
and at last he had reached
the top of the tree.
He stopped to catch his breath.

Looking up he saw his best
friend,
the beautiful Christmas tree
fairy,
who looked more
glittery and
sparkly
than ever before.
She smiled her biggest smile
and stretched out her arms to
greet him.

But outside the sun had started to rise, it was now
Christmas Day morning!
It was too late!

The Snowman and the Christmas tree fairy
had frozen still.

TOWN HALL

They could now feel the rumble of children's
feet coming down the stairs.
They could hear their laughter and squeals
of delight as they entered the room.

rumble,
rumble

The children ran over to the tree
and began to pass around all the
Christmas presents.

Except one little boy who had noticed the Christmas tree fairy and the Snowman at the top of the tree.

They were looking at each other, the fairy's arms were
stretched out as though she wanted to hug the Snowman.

The little boy picked up the Snowman and moved him
into the arms of the
Christmas tree fairy.

Did you find the little mice
throughout the story?

19 Little mice

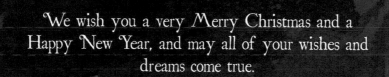

We wish you a very Merry Christmas and a Happy New Year, and may all of your wishes and dreams come true.